ISBN 0 86163 081 5

© Award Publications Limited 1983

Spring House, Spring Place

London N.W. 5

Printed in Belgium

TOM THUMB

Illustrated by RENE CLOKE

AWARD PUBLICATIONS — LONDON

TOM THUMB

"How happy we should be if we had a
little son" sighed the farmer's wife.

"Yes," agreed the farmer, "even if he we
little bigger than my thumb."

The fairies must have been listening, for
the next day the farmer found a tiny little
boy sitting on the doorstep.

He was so small that his father had to make him a cradle from a pea-pod and, although he became very clever as he grew older, he never grew any bigger.

So he was named Tom Thumb.

Tom's father and mother were delighted with him; his mother made tiny clothes for him and his father carved pretty little toys from nutshells.

One day,
Tom heard
the farmer wishing
that someone could drive the horse and cart
to the woods where he was collecting logs.

"Let me sit in the horse's ear," cried Tom
"I will say 'Gee-up and whoa' at the right
time and the horse will do as I say."

The farmer laughed but he agreed to
Tom's plan.

So Tom, sitting in the horse's ear, drove the cart to the edge of the wood to meet his father.

He cried "Gee-up" and "Whoa" and the horse understood just which way to go, although it looked as though no one was driving him.

Two men, who were standing in the road, were amazed when they saw Tom's father take the boy from the horse's ear.

"What a clever little fellow!" said one, "we could make a lot of money if we showed him in town."

They tried to buy Tom from the farmer who, at first, said "No" but Tom whispered, "Let me go, I will soon be back again!"

So the farmer took the money and parted with Tom.

"I'll sit on the brim of your hat," said Tom "I should like to have a view of the countryside."

Tom looked around him as the men walked along, taking notice of the way they were going.

That evening, the two men sat down to rest and while they were talking together, the hat, with Tom upon it, was put on the ground.

Tom hopped off and stole away amongst the long grass.

He crept into a nest belonging to a mouse and there he hid, while the angry men searched everywhere for him.

When they had gone away, Tom crept from the hole.

It was night-time and he decided to wait until daylight before starting for home.

"I must find a comfortable place to spend the night," said the boy and was lucky in finding a big empty snail shell.

Curling up in this, he slept until morning and then, following the path he had seen from the brim of the man's hat, he hurried home.

Tom Thumb's
father and mother
were overjoyed to see
him again but it was
not long before he had
another adventure.

Climbing over the rim of a basin his
mother had left on the table, Tom fell into a
pudding mixture.

Before he could cry out, the pudding was
tied in a cloth
and set in a
cooking pot over
the fire.

"Oh dear!" cried Tom's mother, as Tom jumped about, "the pudding is alive!"

She was so frightened that she gave it to a passing tinker.

But he was soon alarmed at the way the pudding behaved and threw it by the wayside.

Tom was able to scramble out and run home again.

"I am going to milk the cows," said the farmer's wife one day, "but if I take Tom with me, I must tie him to a thistle or he will certainly be lost."

This she did and walked off
thinking that Tom would be quite
safe.

Tom sat on the thistle
very happily and talked
to a bee and a
butterfly.

"Perhaps you
could take me for
a ride," he said to
the butterfly.

"Someday,"
laughed the
butterfly,
fluttering off.

But then a cow came up to the thistle and, without noticing Tom, took a large bite.

"Hi! hi!" yelled the little boy, "let me go!"

He danced and kicked in the cow's mouth until the cow was glad to drop him.

One of the toys which the farmer made for his tiny son was a whip from a stem of barley.

Tom was very proud of this and marched about pretending that he had a team of horses.

But a great eagle, seeing a little creature moving on the ground, swooped down and, picking up Tom, flew off with him.

Tom wasn't easy to carry and he fought and wriggled so much that the eagle had to drop him.

Down fell Tom,
down —
down —
and splash into the sea!

Poor Tom Thumb was terrified for he couldn't swim and he sank deeper and deeper into the water.

Just then, a big fish came by and, thinking that Tom looked a tasty morsel, he swallowed him whole.

"Well," thought Tom, "this isn't very comfortable but, at least, I haven't drowned."

It seemed a long time before the fish was suddenly jerked out of the water and Tom realized that it had been caught by a fisherman.

"I will sell this fine fish to the King's cook," said the man and off he went to the Palace with his catch.

The cook was very glad to buy such a fine fish but when he cut it open before cooking it, he dropped his knife in astonishment.

Out popped Tom Thumb!

"I'd better take you to the King" decided the cook.

So he placed Tom on a plate and took him to the royal apartments.

When Tom Thumb saw the King and Queen, he gave a low bow.

"How delightful" laughed the Queen, "we must keep him for the children to play with."

So Tom Thumb became a plaything for
the little princes and princesses.

But, although they were very kind to him and made him a tiny house and some beautiful clothes, Tom was soon tired of being treated like a toy.

"I wish I could go home," he begged.

At last, the King decided that he should have his wish and when Tom had thanked all the royal family, he was taken to the cottage gate by the King's servants.

The farmer and his wife could hardly believe their eyes as Tom came running up the path.

They never tired of hearing his adventures and Tom Thumb lived safely at the farm for the rest of his life.